In memory of my
father and mother
—A.H.B.

To all my friends and my
dearest wife, Tiziana
—J.B.B.

*Library of Congress Cataloging-in-Publication Data*
Benjamin, A. H., date.
Mouse, mole, and the falling star / by A.H. Benjamin; illustrated by John Bendall-Brunello. — 1st American ed.
p. cm.
Summary: The pursuit of a falling star and its fabulous reward almost breaks up the good friendship between Mole and Mouse.
ISBN 0-525-46880-3
[1. Friendship—Fiction. 2. Moles (Animals)—Fiction. 3. Mice—Fiction.
4. Stars—Fiction.] I. Bendall-Brunello, John, ill. II. Title.
PZ7.B43457 Mo 2002 [E]—dc21 2001047142

Published in the United States 2002 by Dutton Children's Books, a division of Penguin Putnam Books for Young Readers
345 Hudson Street, New York, New York 10014 • www.penguinputnam.com

Originally published in Great Britain 2002 by Little Tiger Press, London
Typography by Richard Amari • Printed in Belgium
First American Edition
2 4 6 8 10 9 7 5 3 1

# Mouse, Mole,
## and the Falling Star

by A. H. Benjamin

illustrated by
John Bendall-Brunello

DUTTON CHILDREN'S BOOKS • NEW YORK

Mouse and Mole were
the best of friends.
They had fun together.

They shared everything.

They trusted each other completely, even with
their deepest secrets.

When one was sad or not feeling well, the other was always there to comfort him.

That's how much they loved each other.

"I'm lucky to have a friend like you," Mole would say.

"No," Mouse would reply. "I'm lucky to have a friend like *you!*"

One summer evening, Mole and Mouse lay side by side on top of a hill, gazing at the starry sky.

"Aren't stars beautiful?" sighed Mole happily.

"Yes," said Mouse, "and magic, too. They sometimes fall from the sky, you know. And if you ever find a fallen star, your wishes will come true."

"Wow!" said Mole. "Then you could wish for anything in the world, and you would have it."

"That's right," said Mouse dreamily. "Just imagine that!"

Mole and Mouse fell silent
for a moment, dreaming of
magic stars and all the things
they could wish for.

Just then, a shooting star zipped across the
sky. One moment it was there, and the next it
had gone.

"Did you see that?" gasped Mole, sitting up.

"Yes, I did," cried Mouse. "It's a fallen star, and
I'm going to find it!"

Mouse scrambled to his feet and scurried down the hill.

"Wait!" called Mole, racing after him. "It's my star! I saw it first."

"No, I saw it first!" shouted Mouse. "It's *my* star!"

When they reached the bottom of the hill, Mole
and Mouse started searching for the fallen star.
Each one hoped he would find it first. But
neither did.

Perhaps the star fell in the woods, thought Mouse. I'll go and look for it tomorrow.

Mole stared toward the woods, too. He was thinking exactly the same thing.

But they did not tell each other, and they
went back to their homes without even saying
good night.

The next day before sunrise,
Mole snuck out of his house
and set off toward the woods.

A few minutes later,
Mouse did the same.

Mouse and Mole spent the whole morning
in the woods, looking for the fallen star. Once or
twice they spotted each other. But they pretended
they hadn't.

Then, toward afternoon, Mole came across a small patch of charred grass. Maybe this is where the star had fallen, he thought. But someone's already taken it. It can only be Mouse!

A little later, Mouse came across the same
charred patch of grass. He thought the star had
fallen there, too. "It's gone!" he cried. "And I bet
I know who's taken it. It has to be Mole!"

As darkness fell, both Mole and Mouse made their separate ways home, each feeling very angry with the other. They did not speak to each other again, except to argue.

"You stole my star!" Mole yelled.

"No, you stole my star!" Mouse yelled back.

Mole didn't trust Mouse, and Mouse didn't trust Mole.

So, Mole sneaked into Mouse's house to find the star…

and later Mouse looked
through Mole's window to see
where Mole had hidden it.

But neither found the fallen
star.

The days rolled by, and summer was nearly over. Mole and Mouse grew lonely and miserable. They missed each other's company, the fun they used to have together, the secrets they had shared. They even missed the sad moments.

Mole can keep the star if he wants, thought Mouse. All I want is my friend back.

If I had never seen that star, Mouse would still be my friend, thought Mole.

Soon the fallen star became
just a sad memory—until one
day…

Mouse was climbing the hill when he spotted a golden leaf, swirling and twirling in the air.

"It's the fallen star!" he cried. "Mole must have lost it. I'll catch it for him."

Not far away, Mole noticed Mouse chasing after something that looked like a star.

It's Mouse's star, he thought. I'll help him catch it.

Up and up the hill ran Mole and Mouse, until
they reached the top. But the leaf was already
high in the sky, glimmering in the autumn
sunshine. It swayed this way and that, as if
waving good-bye, and then vanished altogether.

"The star has gone back to the sky," said Mouse.

"That's where it belongs," said Mole.

"Maybe it's for the best," sighed Mouse.

"I'm sure it is," agreed Mole.

There was a moment's silence.

"Anyway, we don't need a star. We have each other," said Mouse.

"Of course we have," agreed Mole.

They gave each other a big hug, and then lay back on top of the hill, feeling the wind. With their arms and legs stretched out, they looked just like two furry stars.